BYE BYE

Margaret Read MacDonald
& Gerald Fierst

Illustrations by Kitty Harvill

Plum Street Publishers, Inc.
LITTLE ROCK

There was a

BIG
BIG
FROG!

And a little little mosquito.

BIG!

Little.

BIG!

Little.

Bye Bye

Mosquito!

There was a

BIG BIG SNAKE!

And a little little frog.

BIG!

Little.

BIG!

Little.

Bye Bye Frog!

There was a

BIG
BIG
BIRD!

And a little little snake.

BIG!

Little.

BIG!

Little.

Bye Bye Snake!

There was a  **BIG**

BIG TIGER!

And a little   little bird.

BIG!

Little.

BIG!

Little.

Bye Bye Bird!

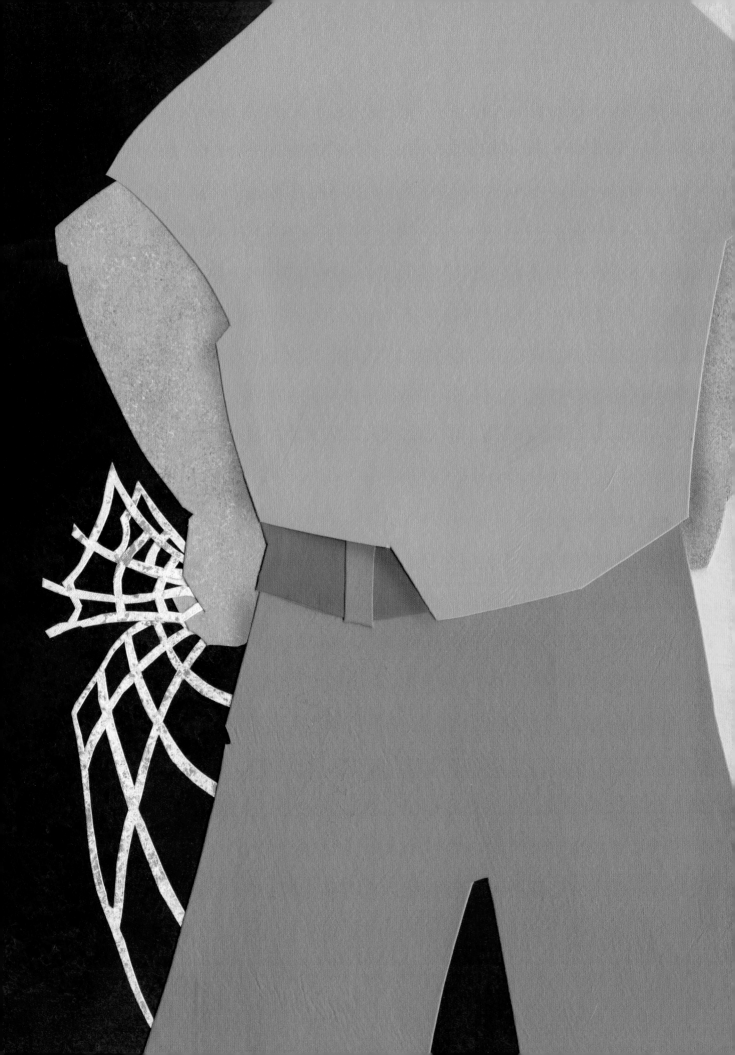

There was a

BIG
BIG
MAN!

And a little little tiger.

BIG!

Little.

BIG!

Little.

There was a

BIG
BIG
MAN!

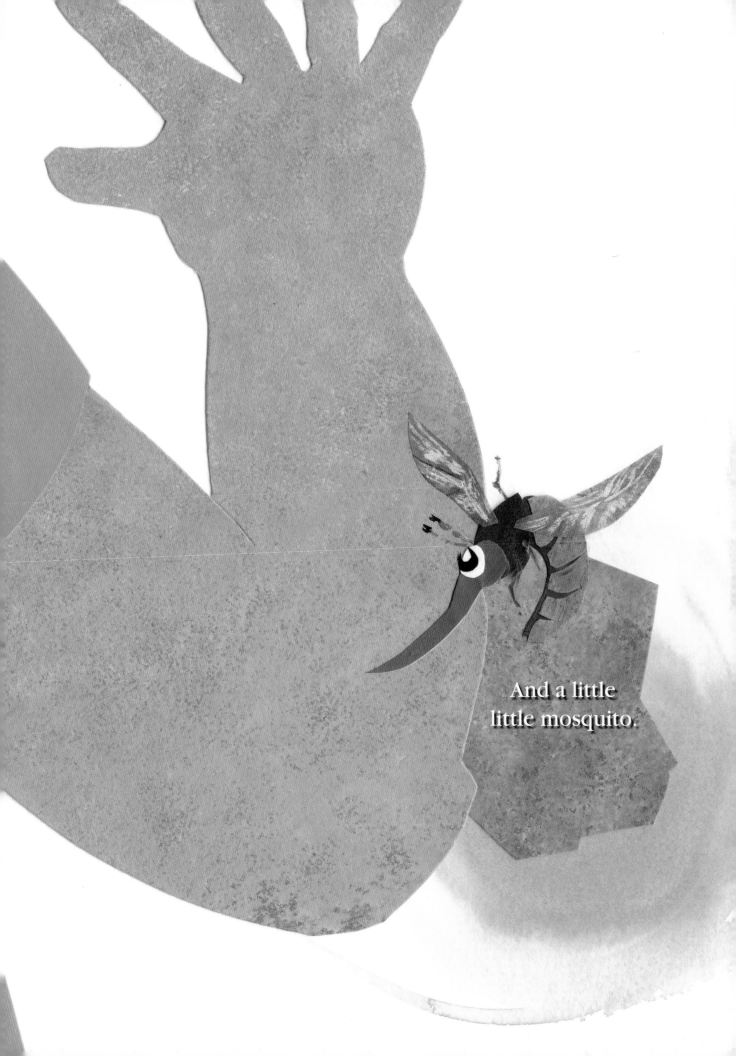

And a little
little mosquito.

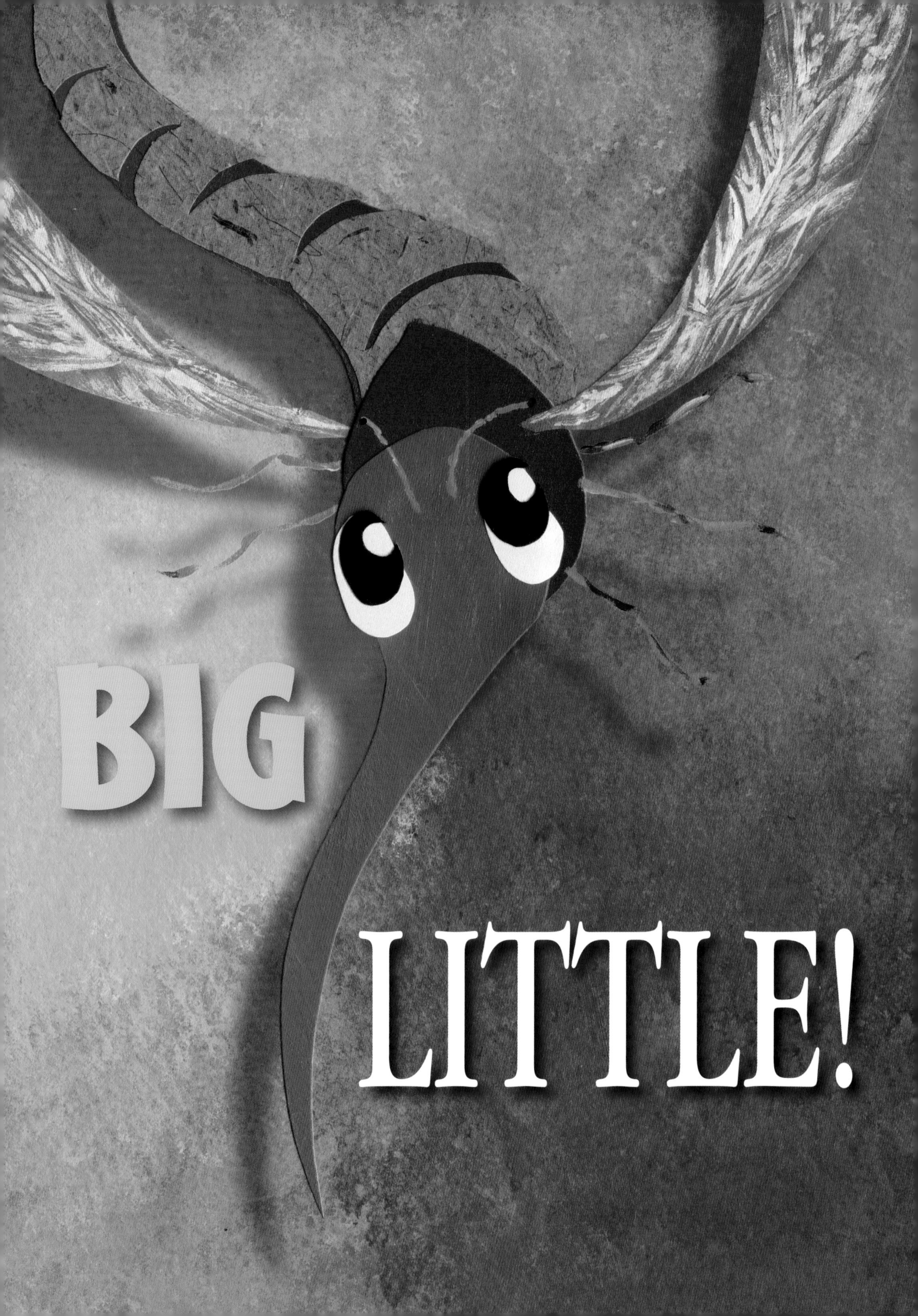
BIG
LITTLE!

For BIG Murray Cormac Martin!
– MRM

To Anjel–little girl, BIG WORLD:
Take a BIG BIG BITE
– GF

For Christoph, my Big BIG LOVE
– KH

Copyright © 2017 by Margaret Read MacDonald and Gerald Fierst

Illustrations copyright © 2017 by Catherine Harvill

Published 2017 by Plum Street Publishers, Inc.,
2701 Kavanaugh Boulevard, Suite 202, Little Rock, Arkansas 72205
www.plumstreetpublishers.com

Book design by Charlie Ross

First Edition

Printed in South Korea by Four Colour Print Group, Louisville, Kentucky
10 9 8 7 6 5 4 3 2 1 HB (ISBN 978-1-945268-03-8)

LIBRARY OF CONGRESS CONTROL NUMBER: 2017936613
The paper used in this publication meets the minimum requirements of
the American National Standards for Information Sciences—
Permanence of Paper for Printed Library Materials,
ANSI/NISO Z39.48–1992.

08/01/2017
79449-0
Printed by We SP Corp., Seoul, S. Korea